Hansel & Gretel

WILL MOSES

Hansel & Gretel

A Retelling from the Original Tale
by the Brothers Grimm

PHILOMEL BOOKS

For Jerry, Lloyd & Georgianna—three pretty good kids!

—W.M.

Dear Reader,

Ever since I began illustrating books for children, I have wanted to illustrate *Hansel and Gretel*. When I was a little boy, it was one of my favorite stories, and many nights, I drifted off to sleep listening to my mother reading this old tale from a version that was printed in a children's magazine of the time. I had those fond memories in my mind when I mentioned to my book editor that *Hansel and Gretel* was a story that I really wanted to try.

However, I confess that when I went back to read the story after so many years had passed by, I wondered if I had chosen well. There are aspects of this story, having to do with the stepmother and father and witch, that are dark. But when I mentioned that I was thinking of illustrating the story to people at book signings and in general conversation, it was apparent that not only were people familiar with the story, but *Hansel and Gretel* struck a chord with just about everyone.

Hansel and Gretel is many things: a cautionary tale, a coming-of-age story, a good-versus-evil narrative of love, survival, hard challenges, and the use of one's wits and courage to overcome adversity. It is also a tale from a long-ago era when the basic realities of survival were considerably harsher than today and perhaps human sensibilities were not as refined.

Hansel and Gretel is a great story that I believe is timeless and strikes each of us at our core. I had a great time creating this book and in so doing, hope that I have helped keep this old tale alive for yet another generation to appreciate.

Will Moses

Long ago there lived a woodcutter, his wife and his children, Hansel and Gretel. The woodcutter's family lived in a little cottage near the edge of an ancient and mysterious forest, and it is in this mysterious old forest that this tale takes place.

My story begins late one moonlit night, while wolves howled nearby, and the wood-cutter's family lay in their beds, hungry and unable to sleep. The woodcutter suddenly turned to his wife. "Oh, wife, what is to become of us?" he asked. "How can we feed our poor children when we barely have enough for ourselves?"

"I'll tell you what I think," his wife, who was the stepmother of the two children, said cruelly. "Tomorrow morning, we will take Hansel and Gretel with us into the forest—the darkest part—we'll build them a fire, and give them one last piece of bread. Then, you and I will pretend to do our work as always, but instead, we will leave the children there, alone, for good!"

"Oh, no!" said the woodcutter, who loved his children. "We can never do such a thing. Wild animals will find them, and that will be their end."

"You fool!" his wife said hotly, her eyes flashing. "It is either that or all of us will certainly perish. You may as well start making ALL of our coffins in the morning."

Still, the woodcutter would not agree, but his wife harangued and argued until, worn down, he gave in and agreed to the horrible deed.

Luckily, the two children were also hungry and unable to sleep that night, and overheard the dark plan. Poor Gretel wept a tide of bitter tears and cried to Hansel, "I fear it is all over for us, Hansel."

"Shush and be still, little sister," whispered Hansel. "I will find a way to save us. You must not worry. Now, please try to sleep."

A little later, when the woodcutter and his wife finally dozed off, brave little Hansel quietly slipped out the cottage door and, in the light of the moon, filled his pockets with the shiny white pebbles that twinkled brightly in the moon glow. Then, quick as a wink, Hansel was back in his bed, but before sleep overtook him, he whispered, "Sleep in peace, my little sister. God has not forsaken us—all will be well."

At sunrise, their stepmother shouted, "Wake up, you lazybones. Today we all go to the forest again." She gave each child a piece of hard bread and said, "Here is your noonday meal. Save it, because there is nothing else."

Gretel put the bread in her apron pockets since Hansel's pockets were filled with pebbles.

Before long, the little group was well on its way to the forest, but after some distance, Hansel stopped to look back and secretly dropped a pebble. This he did again, and again, until the cruel stepmother growled at him, "Hansel, what are you doing?"

"Oh, I am looking at my little white cat, who is sitting on our roof and wants to say good-bye to me."

"You foolish child," she said. "That's not your cat, it's only the morning sun shining on the chimney. Now, pick up your feet and keep up with us."

On they trudged deep into the woods, but all the while, Hansel secretly dropped his little white stones. When they came to a part of the forest where the children had never been before, the woodcutter built a fire, and his wife told Hansel and Gretel to lie down, warm themselves and rest.

She said, "We are going into the forest to chop wood, and when we're finished, we'll come back to get you."

Hansel and Gretel sat by the fire as they had been told to do, and around noon ate their bread. All day, they could hear the comforting sound of an ax chopping wood and believed their father was near. Soon, they fell asleep.

The sound they heard, though, was not an ax but instead, a sapling cleverly tied by their stepmother so as to thump against a hollow tree with every little breeze—sounding, to all who heard it, like chopping!

When the little pair awoke, it was pitch-dark, and the fire was but glowing embers. Gretel began to fret and cry, pleading to Hansel, "How will we ever get home?"

13

He replied confidently, "We will wait. When the moon rises high, I'm sure we'll make our way!"

And soon, the moon did rise, and taking each other by the hand, the two little children began making their way back home. In the glow of the moon, the pebbles shone like tiny beacons, and after a long night of walking, at sunrise Hansel and Gretel arrived back on their cottage doorstep. They knocked on the door to be let in, and when their astonished stepmother swung the door open and saw the two children, she snarled at them, "You wicked children, why did you sleep so long in the forest? We thought you would never come back again."

When their father saw them, though, he was overjoyed, for he had never wanted to abandon his precious children.

or a time after this, life was better, and food seemed more plentiful. The family's worries eased for a while, but soon enough, another famine ravaged the countryside. The woodcutter's family was once again starving.

Just as before, late at night, when everyone was in their beds, the two children lay awake, listening to their father and stepmother talking.

"All our food is gone," the stepmother said. "All we have left is a loaf of bread. When that is gone, we will have nothing. This time we need to take the children farther into the forest, so far that they'll never find their way home again! Otherwise it will be the end of us all."

Hearing this again from his wife saddened the father, for he thought it would be best to share his last bite with his children. His wife, however, roughly scolded him for a fool and continued her vicious tirade until at last the woodcutter found himself agreeing to her cruel plan for a second time.

Once again, after everyone had finally fallen asleep, Hansel rose from his bed, planning to slip out to the cottage yard and collect more white pebbles. However, this time, to his surprise, he found the door locked tight. He was unable to get out!

Nevertheless, he confidently told his little sister, who was crying softly into her pillow, "All will be right, the dear Lord will never forsake us."

Early the next morning, Hansel and Gretel were roused from their beds and given a chunk of bread for their noon meal. Along the way into the woods, Hansel would stop and drop a crumb of his bread to mark the trail.

"Hansel, why are you stopping?" shouted his father. "Keep going."

"Oh, I am looking at my little pigeon, perched on our cottage roof, Father. He wants to say good-bye to me," said Hansel.

"You fool," said his stepmother. "That is only the sun shining on the chimney."

Nevertheless, little by little, Hansel managed to sprinkle crumbs along their path.

Just as before, the two children were led far, far into the forest, to a place they never imagined existed. A fire was lit and the old woman cooed to Hansel and Gretel, "Rest here before the fire, and when the day is done, we will be back to fetch you."

Along about midday, Gretel shared her bread with Hansel, who had used his to mark the path. Before long, the cool air, the warm fire and a little something to eat made the two children sleep. Whey they woke, it was dark and they quickly understood that no one had come for them again.

Hansel comforted his little sister, saying, "We need only wait till the moon rises—just as before, little sister. Then we'll follow our trail of bread crumbs back home. All will be well, don't worry."

When the moon rose, however, no crumbs were to be found anywhere, and Hansel and Gretel soon realized that the birds and animals that live in the forest had happily eaten all their bread!

"Don't fret, we'll find our way," said Hansel, a little less certain than before. But try as they might, they could not find any of the familiar landmarks that might show them the way home.

On the two little children walked, throughout the night and all the next day. They were still no closer to home, though, and by now they were so very hungry and their legs were so very tired that all they could do was lie down on the mossy ground and sleep.

On the third morning of their sad adventure, Hansel and Gretel were ready to give up all hope, when they saw a beautiful snow-white bird sitting on a branch. The bird sang such a sweet song and was so beautiful that the two children agreed to follow it as it flew away.

Into the forest the bird lured them, until suddenly they came to a large clearing. In the middle of the clearing, to their astonishment, was a beautiful gingerbread house, complete with sugar crystal windows and decorated with candy treats and frosting.

"What a blessed meal!" said Hansel. "Let's have a taste. I'll try some delicious candy cane decorations. Gretel, you have some of the sugar crystal window, it looks so very sweet and tasty."

And that is just what the two children did, and who can blame them, since they were both starving!

Hansel broke off a piece of the gingerbread and Gretel began nibbling on the window-panes, when suddenly they heard a sharp voice cry out from within the house:

"Nibble, nibble, I hear a mouse.
Who's nibbling on my house?"

The children answered back:

" 'Tis the wind, the wind; it's very mild,
Blowing like the Heavenly Child."

The two children continued to enjoy the feast, as they were so hungry and the house tasted ever so good to them. Hansel pulled down another large chunk of candy cane, and Gretel cracked out a large piece of sugar crystal and ate it with delight.

Suddenly, the door of the house opened and a very old woman, leaning on a crutch, came slinking from within. Hansel and Gretel, quite naturally, were so frightened that they both dropped what they were eating.

"Oh, you poor dear children, what has brought you here, I wonder? Won't you come inside and stay with me? No one is going to harm you," the old woman said sweetly. Then she led them both by the hand into her house, where she served them a fine meal of pancakes, apples, milk and nuts.

Afterward she made up two beds with fine white sheets whereupon Hansel and Gretel lay down and were soon asleep.

In truth, though, the old woman was wicked and only pretended to be nice. She was, in fact, an evil, nasty witch, always on the lookout for little lost children. She had built her clever gingerbread house to lure boys and girls, and as soon as she had the poor lost children in her power, the evil old thing would cook and eat them!

Now, this old witch had poor eyesight and had trouble making her way about, but she more than made up for this with an animal-like ability to smell. She had known from scenting the wind that Hansel and Gretel were near long before they saw her house, and so had plenty of time to prepare her trap.

Early the next morning, hovering above the rosy-cheeked children as they lay sleeping, the old witch thought to herself, What a tasty meal these two would make! Quickly, she grabbed Hansel in her bony hands and carried him away to a special pen with a locking door.

He screamed and yelled but it didn't matter, for she was surprisingly powerful and heartless. The old hag then went back and shook Gretel awake, screeching at her: "Get up, you lazybones, get up. You need to fetch water to cook your brother something nice to eat."

Cackling, she said, "He's in my fattening pen, and when he's fat enough, I'm going to eat him!"

Poor Gretel burst out with hot tears, but it was no use. She had to do what the witch commanded or it would be the end of them both then and there. So, for several days the very best food was cooked for Hansel while Gretel got nothing but boiled crab shells.

Every morning, the old witch skulked over to the cage where she kept Hansel penned and shouted to him: "Hansel, stick out your finger so I can see how fat you've grown."

However, Hansel was a bright boy and soon realized the old witch could not see very well. So, every morning, he stuck out an old thin bone that he had found in his pen for the witch to inspect.

The witch was fooled by the trick. In fact, she was puzzled over why Hansel didn't seem to fatten up.

After a month had passed and Hansel appeared no fatter than the day she put him in the pen, the evil old witch flew into a rage and decided to wait no longer!

"Gretel!" she cackled. "Get me some wood for the fire. Fat or thin, Hansel is going to be my supper feast!"

Oh, how Gretel wailed and cried as she carried buckets of water and armloads of wood for a cooking fire. "If only the wild beasts in the forest had gotten us," she cried, "then we could have gone to heaven together."

"First, though, we'll bake bread!" barked the old witch. "Already I have heated the oven and kneaded the dough." All the while she was saying this, she was gently coaxing Gretel toward the oven, where hot flames danced from the fire within.

"Now, Gretel," the old witch sweetly murmured. "Dear girl, you crawl inside and see that the oven is properly warmed."

Of course, the old hag intended to slam the oven door on Gretel and cook her, too! Sensing what the evil old thing was up to, Gretel pretended not to understand what the witch wanted from her. Gretel said, "How, please, am I to do what you ask? I am just a small girl and don't know how to get into an oven."

"You foolish goose," the old woman snapped. "It's simple enough! Watch, even an old woman like me can climb in!"

And with that, she waddled to the oven, leaned into it . . . and quick as a wink, and with all of her might, Gretel gave the witch a mighty shove, sending the hag tumbling headlong into the fire!

With a bang, Gretel slammed the iron doors shut and bolted them tight, whereupon a great plume of black, oily smoke and terrible howls rose up from the chimney.

Gretel ran straight to Hansel, shouting, "The witch is gone, the old hag is cooked to death and will bother us no more!" With that, Gretel unlocked Hansel's pen and out he popped, hugging and kissing his little sister as they both danced about the yard, shouting, "We're free, we're free, the wicked old witch is dead."

Now that the witch was gone, they had nothing to fear from her. So Hansel and Gretel went to the witch's house and found what they suspected: witch's treasure! Gold, pearls, rubies, emeralds and diamonds overflowing from her hoard of treasure chests.

"These are much better than pebbles," said a grinning Hansel as he filled his pockets with treasure. And Gretel, too, stuffed her pockets with dazzling jewels.

Later, their pockets brimming with jewels, and having eaten their fill from the witch's pantry, Hansel and Gretel decided it was time to get out of the witch's forest, and they began to find their way home. When they came to a broad river that seemed to offer no way across, Hansel said, "I can not see any bridges or boats that might take us to the other side."

"Don't worry, Hansel," said Gretel. "Look, there is an elegant white duck swimming over there. She's bound to help us, if only we ask her." So Gretel sweetly called out:

"Help us, help us, beautiful duck!
We are Hansel and Gretel and out of luck.
We can't get across the river, try as we may,
Won't you please help us, this fine day?"

Sure enough, the kind and handsome duck swam over to them and carried each child to the other side of the river, whereupon Gretel gave the duck a generous piece of gingerbread from the witch's house.

The little travelers walked on for two more days till suddenly the forest and land became more and more familiar, and to their amazement, late one afternoon, they caught sight of their own cottage.

Hansel and Gretel began to run, and before long, burst through the cottage door and threw themselves about their father with hugs and kisses.

The overjoyed woodcutter had not had a single happy minute since leaving his children in the woods, and in the meanwhile, his wife had died from what the doctor declared to be a black heart.

Upon hearing this news, Gretel shook out her apron and let loose all the riches it held, and Hansel emptied his pockets of treasure, tossing it before his astonished father. Their troubles were at last over.

Now, with their newfound good fortune and the love of each other, the woodcutter and his children lived out the rest of their lives in happiness and peace.

Like a mouse caught by a cat, my tale is finished! Sleep well tonight, and don't let this old story give you a fright. Your parents love you dear and will never let harm come near!

Patricia Lee Gauch, Editor

PHILOMEL BOOKS
A division of Penguin Young Readers Group.   Published by The Penguin Group.
Penguin Group (USA) Inc., 375 Hudson Street, New York, NY 10014, U.S.A.
Penguin Group (Canada), 90 Eglinton Avenue East, Suite 700, Toronto, Ontario, Canada M4P 2Y3 (a division of Pearson Penguin Canada Inc.)
Penguin Books Ltd, 80 Strand, London WC2R 0RL, England.
Penguin Ireland, 25 St. Stephen's Green, Dublin 2, Ireland (a division of Penguin Books Ltd.)
Penguin Group (Australia), 250 Camberwell Road, Camberwell, Victoria 3124, Australia (a division of Pearson Australia Group Pty Ltd).
Penguin Books India Pvt Ltd, 11 Community Centre, Panchsheel Park, New Delhi - 110 017, India.
Penguin Group (NZ), Cnr Airborne and Rosedale Roads, Albany, Auckland 1310, New Zealand (a division of Pearson New Zealand Ltd).
Penguin Books (South Africa) (Pty) Ltd, 24 Sturdee Avenue, Rosebank, Johannesburg 2196, South Africa.
Penguin Books Ltd, Registered Offices: 80 Strand, London WC2R 0RL, England.

Design by Semadar Megged.   Text set in 15-point Goudy.   The art was done in oil on Fabriano paper.

Library of Congress Cataloging-in-Publication Data
Moses, Will.   Hansel and Gretel / Will Moses.   p. cm.
Summary: A retelling of the well-known tale in which two children lost in the woods find their way home despite
an encounter with a wicked witch.
[1. Fairy tales. 2. Folklore—Germany.] I. Hansel and Gretel. English. II. Title.
PZ8.M8465Han 2006   398.2'0943'02—dc22   2004015740
ISBN 0-399-24234-1
1 3 5 7 9 10 8 6 4 2
First Impression